THE GREAT WALL OF CHINA

CARMEL REILLY

Australia • Brazil • Japan • Korea • Mexico • Singapore • Spain • United Kingdom • United States

The Great Wall of China

Fast Forward
Emerald Level 25

Text: Carmel Reilly
Editor: Johanna Rohan
Design: Ami Sharpe
Series design: James Lowe
Production controller: Seona Galbally
Photo research: Gillian Cardinal
Audio recordings: Juliet Hill, Picture Start
Spoken by: Matthew King and Abbe Holmes
Reprint: Jennifer Foo

Acknowledgements
The author and publisher would like to acknowledge permission to reproduce material from the following sources:
Front cover: Getty Images
Back cover: iStockphoto
AAP Image/AP Photo, p 22; AAP Image/AFP Photo/ESA, p 7 bottom; akg-images, p 13 top, Bruce Connolly/14, 16; Art Archive, The/British Library, p 12; Getty Images, p 18 centre, 21 -1, 23; Jupiterimages, p 4 left, 8 bottom right, 18 bottom right; Jupiterimages Corporation © 2007, p 6, 9 left; Lonely Planet Images Maps/Lonely Planet Images, p 4; Photolibrary, pp 5, 7 top, 8 centre, 9 right, 10, 11, 13 bottom right, 15, 17, 19.

ISBN 978 0 17 012726 4
ISBN 978 0 17 012717 6 (set)

Cengage Learning Australia
Level 7, 80 Dorcas Street
South Melbourne, Victoria Australia 3205
Phone: 1300 790 853

Cengage Learning New Zealand
Unit 4B Rosedale Office Park
331 Rosedale Road, Albany, North Shore NZ 0632
Phone: 0508 635 766

For learning solutions, visit cengage.com.au

Printed in Australia by Ligare Pty Ltd
8 9 10 11 12 13 14 22 21 20 19 18

THE UNIVERSITY OF MELBOURNE

Evaluated in independent research by staff from the Department of Language, Literacy and Arts Education at the University of Melbourne.

THE GREAT WALL OF CHINA

CARMEL REILLY

Contents

Chapter 1

MY TRIP TO CHINA

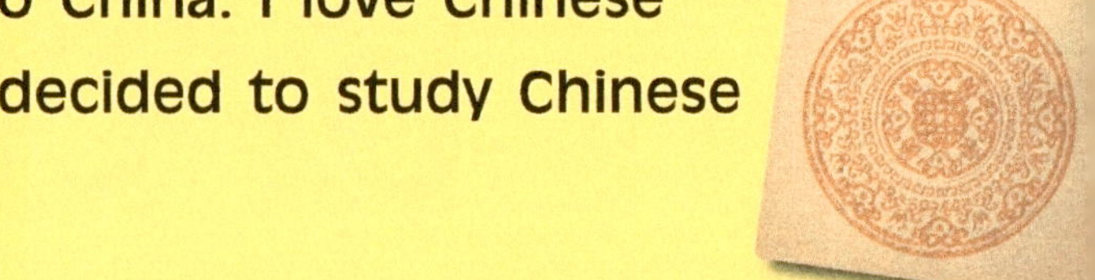

I've always wanted to travel to China. I love Chinese art and food, and this year, I decided to study Chinese language at school.

As a part of our studies, a small group of us visited China with two of our teachers. We had the best time! The highlight of my trip was visiting the Great Wall of China.

RUSSIA
MONGOLIA
Ürümqi
The Great Wall
BEIJING
Yinchuan
Tianjin
Xining
Lanzhou
Zhengzhou
Xi'an
Nanjing
Chengdu
Wuhan
Hangzhou
China
Fuzhou
Kunming
Nanning
Guangzhou
Taiwan
Macau
Hong Kong
VIETNAM
LAOS
Haikou

Beijing

the Simatai part of the Great Wall

We arrived in Beijing (pronounced: *Bay-jing*) and travelled to Simatai, which is one of the parts of the Great Wall that is close by. It took us a few hours to reach Simatai by bus from the centre of the city.

Chapter 2

THE GREAT WALL

The Great Wall of China is the longest man-made structure on Earth. Although a lot of the wall has now fallen into ruin, what is left covers a distance of more than 4000 kilometres across the north of China. It runs from the Yellow Sea in the east, curves around the north of Beijing and ends up in Xinjiang (pronounced *Shin-gee-ang*) province far in the west.

The Great Wall can be seen from space. This is a photo taken by a satellite showing a part of the Great Wall northeast of Beijing.

The Great Wall is also seen as an important historical site and was placed on the UNESCO World Heritage List in 1987.

Chapter 3

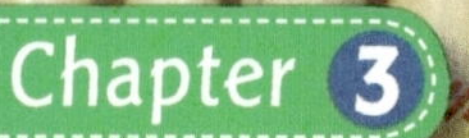

VISITING THE WALL

When I first saw the Great Wall, I was amazed at its size. I tried to imagine how something so big and impressive could have been built so long ago.

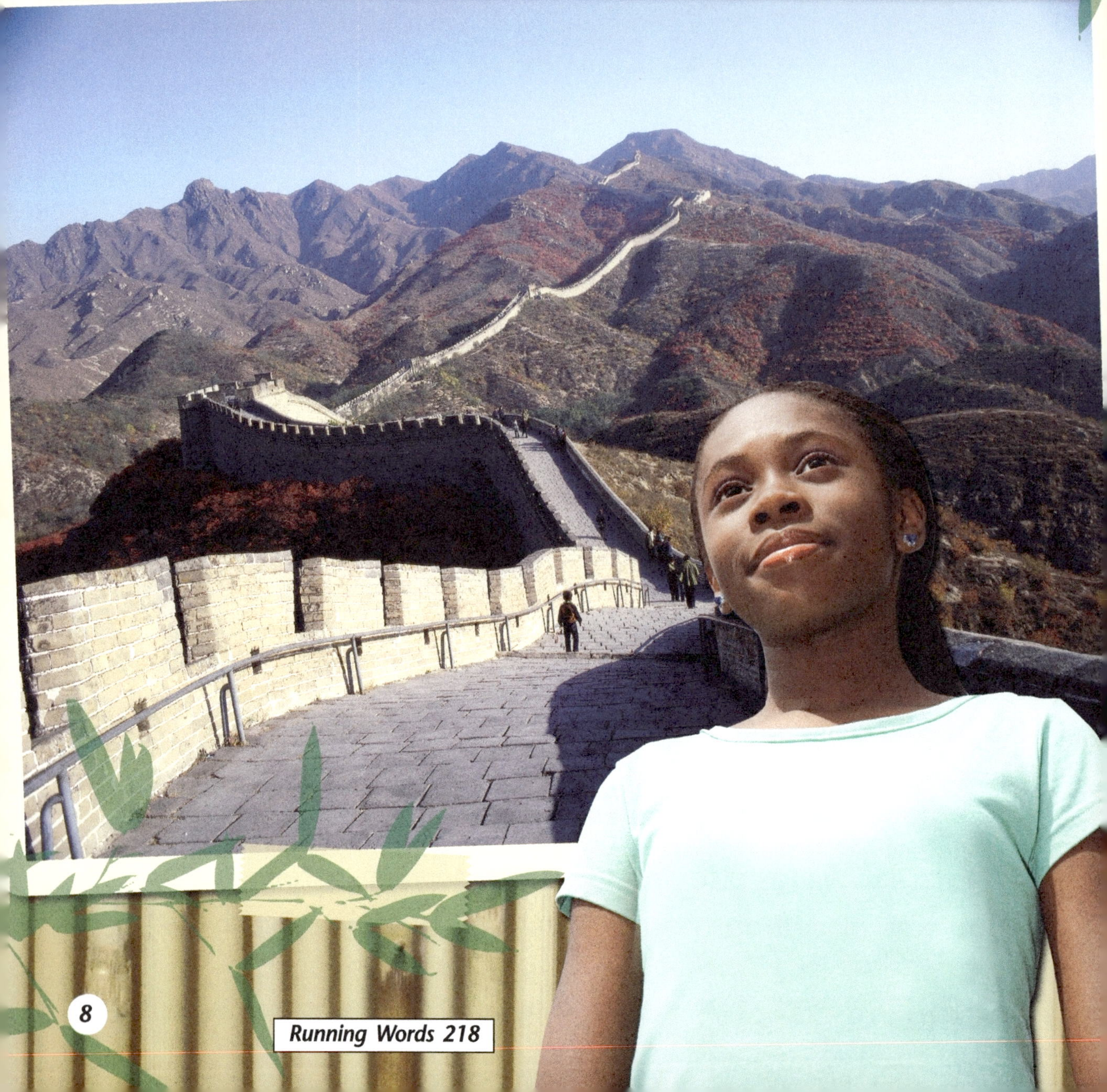

Running Words 218

The Great Wall is very high and it's quite wide, too. It was built like this so that soldiers could walk along it to get from one section to another. It's wide enough in places to allow small carts to travel along the walkway at the top. The army would use these walkways to carry food and weapons between the watchtowers where the soldiers were stationed. Today, these walkways carry thousands of tourists each day.

Chapter 4

THE HISTORY OF THE GREAT WALL

We had a guide called Ran to take us along part of the Great Wall and tell us about its history. Ran started by telling us that Chinese civilisation is the most long-lasting civilisation in history. It began about 3000 years ago.

Ran

Emperor Qianlong (1711–1799)

In China's imperial period (220 BC to 1912 AD), China was ruled by a series of emperors under 11 different **dynasties.** During this time, the Chinese built a strong, stable government and social system that helped to keep their civilisation peaceful and well ordered. Part of the reason they were able to do this was because China was isolated from Western civilisations. However, every now and then, **nomadic** invaders would try to attack China, and this is why the first Great Wall was built.

The Qin Dynasty

The first of the great walls in the north of China was built in the Qin (pronounced: *Chin*) dynasty by the emperor Shi Huangdi (pronounced: *She Hwang-dee*), in about 200 BC. Shi Huangdi thought a huge wall was necessary to defend the Chinese empire against invaders from the north.

Emperor Shi Huangdi

In order to build the wall, Shi Huangdi forced his people to work on it. They had to work very hard, and many of them lost their lives because of accidents and illness.

Emperor Shi Huangdi is also famous for the tomb he built for himself. He filled it with thousands of life-sized terracotta soldiers to guard him in the afterlife.

Other Dynasties

Emperors from later dynasties also built long walls to stop invaders. Almost all of these walls were made from earth, sticks and rocks rammed together. Most of these early walls have crumbled away because they weren't made from very solid materials.

the remains of the Great Wall at Yichuan

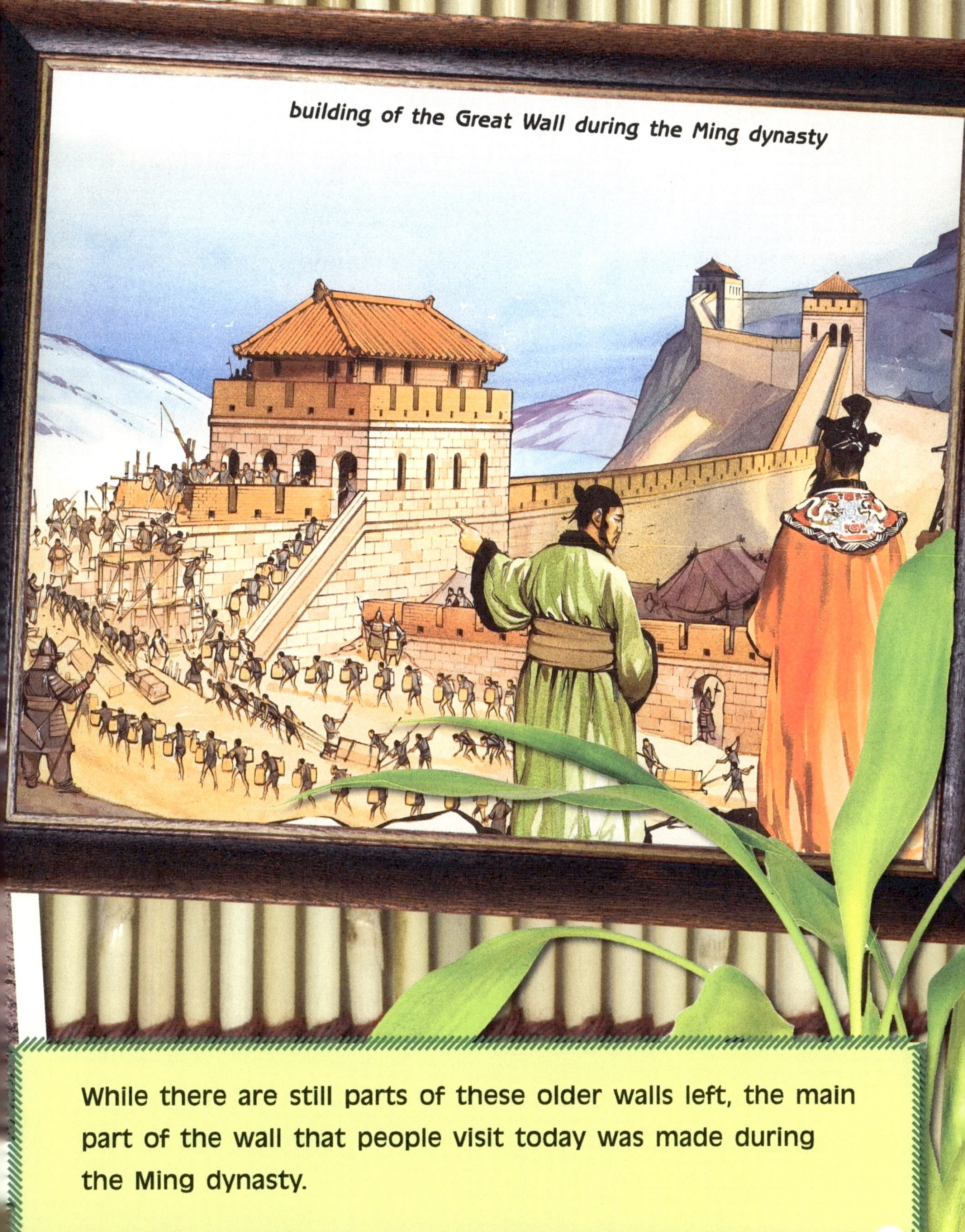
building of the Great Wall during the Ming dynasty

While there are still parts of these older walls left, the main part of the wall that people visit today was made during the Ming dynasty.

The Ming Dynasty

The part of the wall nearest to Beijing was built during the Ming dynasty (1368 AD to 1644 AD).

It had first been erected to stop raids from the **Mongol people** from the west. Later, more was added to block the Manchu people from the north.

Emperor Chu Yuan-Chung, founder of the Ming Dynasty

The wall that was built in the Ming dynasty was very impressive. Much of it was made from brick on the outside, and its centre was filled with earth. However, the wall didn't keep out the invaders. In the end, the Ming dynasty fell to the Manchu. The Manchu went on to create their own dynasty in China and to extend their territory past the wall far to the north.

THE WALL AS A SYMBOL

As Ran told us about the history of the Great Wall, I wondered if all the money and time spent building the walls had been worth it. I asked Ran what she thought.

"Many people say the walls weren't just for defence," Ran said. "They say the walls were symbols of the strength and power of the Chinese empire at the time. The wall was the Chinese border, and when outsiders reached it, they were able to see that a rich and powerful civilisation lay behind it. It was sending them a message not to come any further."

Dragons

I thought about Ran's words as I looked along the **ramparts.** I was impressed by what I saw, and I was sure that nomadic people centuries ago would have been impressed, too.

I looked at the wall that followed the ridge of the hills to the west, and it reminded me of a dragon rising up from the ground. Dragons are one of the most powerful symbols of good luck and greatness in China. They are also a symbol of China and the Chinese people themselves.

Chapter 6

THE WALL TODAY

As I looked at the hundreds of tourists crowded along the wall, I thought Ran was right about the wall being a symbol. But now that symbol's meaning has changed.

For hundreds of years, the Great Wall of China was used to keep people away from China, but these days it brings many visitors to the country. These days, China no longer wants to keep people out. It welcomes business and tourism, and a greater understanding of its culture. What better place to do this than at the Great Wall?

Glossary

dynasties successions of rulers who belong to the same family for generations

Mongol people native people from Mongolia

nomadic people who move from place to place

ramparts walls

Index